In the Garden

Written by Mitch Cronick

Illustrated by Melanie Sharp

◌ Collins

In the tent.

2

3

In the sandpit.

5

In the grass.

In the leaves.

8

9

In the mud.

11

In the bath!

13

A story map

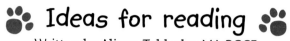

Ideas for reading

Written by Alison Tyldesley MA PGCE
Education, Childhood and Inclusion Lecturer

Learning objectives: reading familiar words; developing strategies to decode unfamiliar words; understanding story elements – character, sequence of events; being aware of actions and reactions in a story; attempting writing for various purposes, e.g. labels; retelling a story; using talk to organise ideas.

Curriculum links: Personal Social and Emotional Development: Responding to experiences, showing a range of feelings;

Knowledge and Understanding of the World: Finding out about your environment; Creative Development: Using imagination in art and design

High frequency words: in, the

Interest words: tent, sandpit, grass, leaves, mud, bath

Word count: 18

Getting started

- Look at the front cover together. Encourage the children to read the title and point to each word.

- Walk through the book looking at the pictures. Leave pp12-15 until later. Ask the children what they think will happen next.

- Ask them to find the interest words on each page (*tent, sandpit, grass, leaves, mud, bath*). What helps them to read the words? Encourage the use of different cues such as the illustration and initial letters.

- Look at the pictures on the right hand page and discuss what Mum is doing. What do they think Mum is saying on p11? Why?

Reading and responding

- Read the book together from the beginning to p13. As the children read, prompt and praise correct reading of familiar words. Prompt the children to use a range of cues to read the interest words.

- Prompt and praise comments on the children's actions and Mum's reactions.

- Did they predict what would happen in the end? Were the children in trouble?